W9-CMS-790

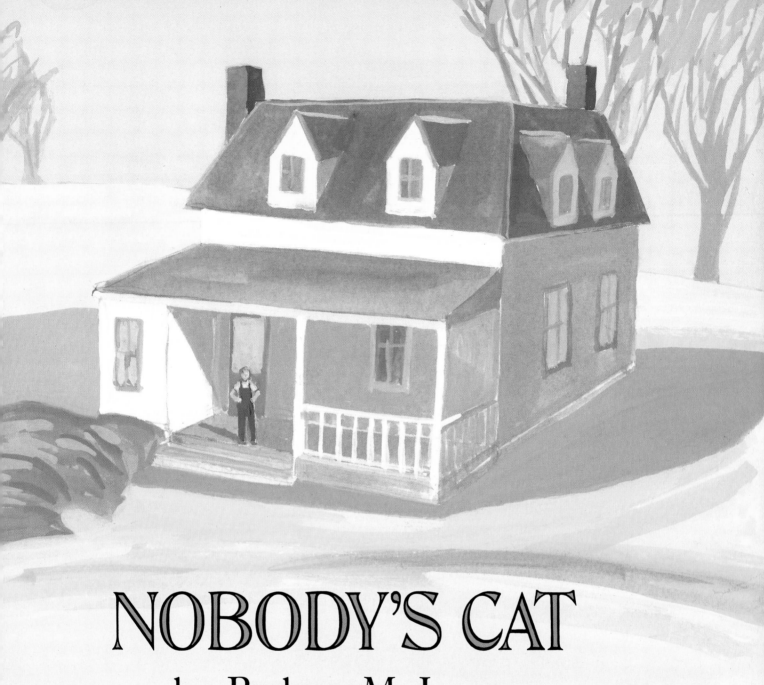

NOBODY'S CAT

by Barbara M. Joosse
pictures by Marcia Sewall

HarperCollins*Publishers*

Nobody's Cat
Text copyright © 1992 by Barbara M. Joosse
Illustrations copyright © 1992 by Marcia Sewall
Printed in the U.S.A. All rights reserved.
Typography by Al Cetta
1 2 3 4 5 6 7 8 9 10
First Edition

Library of Congress Cataloging-in-Publication Data
Joosse, Barbara M.
  Nobody's cat / by Barbara M. Joosse ; pictures by Marcia Sewall.
    p.   cm.
  Summary: A starving cat who has been living in the wild seeks food
and shelter for her kittens and herself by going to the
home of a learning disabled boy.
  ISBN 0-06-020834-1. — ISBN 0-06-020835-X (lib. bdg.)
  1. Feral cats—Juvenile fiction. [1. Feral cats—Fiction.
2. Cats—Fiction.] I. Sewall, Marcia, ill. II. Title.
PZ10.3.J787No   1992   91-37619
[E]—dc20   CIP
                                                    AC

For Phil Hamilton,
whose friendship and medical wizardry
gave us Robby.
I'll never forget.
—B.M.J.

To Little One, Gus Gus, Sam, Itty Bit,
Schnaggle, Little Lady,
and The White Pet
—all strays.
—M.S.

THE FERAL CAT didn't belong to anyone. She had short, mottled fur. There were burdocks in it, and they jabbed at her skin when she moved. Her skin stretched across her bones. She was hungry.

Mew mew meeew! Her babies were hungry, too. The feral cat lay down and offered her milk. The kittens lapped and smacked at the milk. They pumped her breasts with their soft, little paws. When the milk was gone they mewed for more. But there wasn't any.

The mornings were crisp now, and the nest was not so warm. Soon it would be winter. What would they do? The feral cat curled around her babies and nudged them into a warm little ball. They slept.

The next morning, while dew glimmered on the spiderwebs and the sun fought its way through the fog, the feral cat went to the people's house. It had been a long time since she had been near people. Her heart thumped against her chest.

Meeeiow! Meeeiow!

The door opened and a boy came out. The boy crouched down. He was so close, the feral cat could feel the heat of his hand. She wanted to run, but she did not. The boy laid his hand on the feral cat. His hand felt sticky and heavy.

"Mama, there's a cat out here, and it's crying!" The boy spoke slowly, as if it took him a long time to find the right words.

Another voice, a woman's, came from inside. "Yes, Hubbel. The wash is outside, and it's drying."

"No! I said there's a CAT out here," the boy said slowly.

The woman came out, wiping her hands on her apron.

"Can we keep her, Mama?"

"No, Hubbel. This is a wild cat. She's used to living outdoors. Probably some town people didn't want her anymore and dropped her off in the country. I don't think she'll ever trust people again."

Mmmmraaow.

The woman bent over the feral cat. "Why, she's skin and bones! I suppose it wouldn't hurt to put out a dish of cream."

"Can I get it?" asked the boy.

"No, I'm afraid you'll spill it. I might as well."

The woman put out a dish of thick, white cream and returned inside.

The feral cat sniffed inside the dish. It smelled of the woman, but it smelled rich and tasty, too. She began to lap up the cream. She lapped and lapped as if she would never stop. Soon the cream was gone. The cat had licked the dish clean with her raspy tongue.

Mmmraaiow. The feral cat leaned against the boy. She curled her tail softly around his leg, and then she left. The boy was alone on the porch.

When the feral cat returned to the nest, she lay carefully on her side. The people's cream had become milk for her babies. They drank until their bellies were round. Then the feral cat took the tiger-striped kitten and licked it until it was sleek and glossy. She picked it up in her mouth and carried it to the porch.

There was another dish of cream! The feral cat sniffed it. This time it smelled of the boy. She shared the cream with the tiger, and then she told it to wait on the porch without her. The feral cat hid behind the honeysuckle bush.

The kitten cried piteously until the door opened.

"Mama, it's a kitten," called the boy. He searched the yard with his eyes. When he didn't find what he was looking for, he bent over the kitten.

The woman said, "Look at this tiny kitten! What kind of people would make a kitten like this fend for itself?"

The boy grabbed the kitten's front paws and started to lift it up.

"Hubbel." The woman took the kitten out of the boy's arms. "You have to support a kitten with your hand. It hurts them to be picked up by the legs." The woman cradled the kitten in her arms.

The boy pulled the kitten onto *his* lap and tried to cradle it the way the woman had. But the kitten squirmed. It was so small that it did not feel snug in the boy's arms.

"Would you like to keep this kitten, Hubbel?" the woman asked.

The boy searched the yard again. "No," he said haltingly.

"Well, I'm sure we can find a home for such a sweet little thing," said the woman. "I'll make some phone calls."

The feral cat waited behind the honeysuckle bush. Soon a man with a beard rode a bicycle up the sidewalk. He climbed the steps to the porch and rang the bell. The woman showed him the tiger kitten. He held the little thing close to his face and ran his bearded chin along its back. Perhaps the kitten would think the man's beard felt soft, like its mother. The tiger would be happy with this man. When the man put the tiger in his bicycle pouch, the feral cat turned to leave. She did not want to watch her baby ride away.

The feral cat returned to the nest. Her babies mewed eagerly when they saw her. She had been gone a long time, and they were afraid. The babies huddled close against her until the sun settled into the trees.

The feral cat returned to the porch the next morning, and the next. Each time, she brought a kitten. She drank her fill of the cream, sharing a last meal with her kitten. Then she left the kitten there, so the people would find it a home.

On the fourth morning, all the kittens were gone.

Now the nest, in the thin light of autumn, seemed empty and quiet. So the next day the feral cat returned to the porch. She drank the dish of cream. It smelled like the boy.

When she was finished, the feral cat hid behind the honeysuckle bush. The boy came outside and picked up the empty dish. Then he searched the yard again. The boy held very still and waited. He did not move, not even when the woman called him. What was he waiting for?

The feral cat crept from behind the bush to get a better look. The boy turned and looked at her. He smiled, and it seemed to the feral cat as though the sun was brighter now.

The boy waited for the feral cat to climb the stairs. He waited until she came to him and rubbed against his leg. When he bent down to pick her up, she let him. She lay quite still, cradled in his arms, and found that she fit just right.

Then the boy and the cat went inside. They found a basket, and the boy put his soft bathrobe in it. The cat crawled inside. Her new nest was safe and warm. She bunched up her back and stretched her legs. Her eyes felt heavy, so she closed them. Soon she was sleeping.

Now nobody's cat belonged to someone. She wasn't wild anymore.

BARBARA M. JOOSSE is the author of many books for young children and middle grade readers. Her picture books include DINAH'S MAD, BAD WISHES; JAM DAY; and MAMA, DO YOU LOVE ME? Ms. Joosse lives in Hartford, Wisconsin, where one day a wild cat showed up at her door, crying for food. She gave it some, and day by day, one by one, the cat's babies appeared on her front porch. Ms. Joosse and her family found homes for both the mother and her kittens, and she was inspired to write NOBODY'S CAT.

MARCIA SEWALL has illustrated over forty books for children, including THISTLE by Walter Wangerin, Jr., a *School Library Journal* Best Book of 1983; STONE FOX by John Reynolds Gardiner, a *New York Times* Outstanding Children's Book of 1980; and THE BIRTHDAY TREE by Paul Fleischman. Ms. Sewall is also a writer, and in 1986 her book THE PILGRIMS OF PLIMOTH won the *Boston Globe–Horn Book* Award. The sequel to that book, PEOPLE OF THE BREAKING DAY, tells the story of the Wampanoag people, a tribe of Native Americans. She lives in Dorchester, Massachusetts.